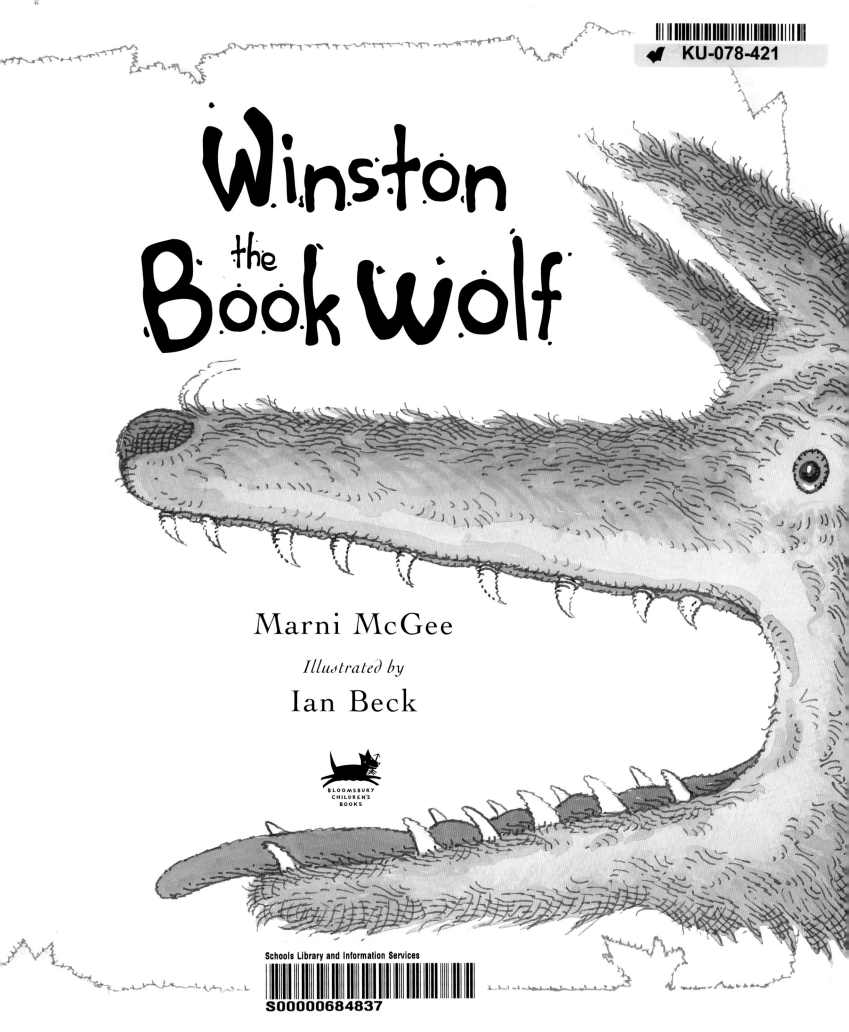

Winston
the
Book Wolf

Marni McGee

Illustrated by

Ian Beck

BLOOMSBURY
CHILDREN'S
BOOKS

Winston the Wolf swished his tail as he trotted past the burger stand. He *did* slow down to sniff, but he did not drool.

Meaty treats were not what Winston had in mind. Winston wanted **books** and he knew where to find them.

He sauntered up the library steps and saw a handwritten sign.
"Words!" he exclaimed. "Yum!"

NO
WOLVES
ALLOWED

He snatched the sign and ate it.

The fierce librarian jingled her bell.
"He's back," she cried,
"that wicked wolf who chews on books!"

Library helpers came running. Winston tried to dodge them, but soon everyone was chasing poor Winston the Wolf.

Winston leaped over computers, hopped over tables and chairs.

Soon he'd be **trapped**

But then a girl named Rosie appeared.
"Quick," she said. "Follow me."
Rosie showed Winston a secret door.

Exit

She led him through an alley, then under a bridge and over a hill.

When at last the two of them
stopped, Rosie demanded the truth.
"Why do you nibble on books?
Why ask for trouble, Wolf?"

"Isn't it obvious? Can you not guess?"
asked Winston. "Words are **so** delicious!
Why, words taste better than roasted
skunk, even better than gopher stew!"

"Wolf," said Rosie,
"you must break this terrible
habit. You must never nibble
on books. Never again,
do you hear?"

Winston began to howl.
"I'll starve," he wailed.
"I'll *die* without words!"

Rosie just laughed. "Oh, hush up, Wolf, and listen to me. You do *not* have to **chew** on a book to taste the lovely words inside. Words taste **even** better when you eat them with your eyes!"

Winston squinted at Rosie.

"Is this a **trick**? Can this be **true**?"

"Trust me," said Rosie. "Sit down. You and I are going to have **lessons.**"

So each afternoon, Rosie read **stories** to Winston.
She taught him to sound out the words.
Winston caught on fast. He learned to eat words with
his eyes, which is to say: Winston learned to **read**!

The hungry wolf ate all sorts of words –
sweet and juicy words

like sunset

and swoosh

and rambunctious.

He wolfed down words like

trickle, icicle

and *twice*.

To him they tasted like clean, spring rain.

His favourite words rhymed with *crunch* —

punch and *munch* and *lunch*.

Winston read Rosie's books until he knew them all by heart. Then Winston said to Rosie:

"I **must** have a new stack of books."

Rosie sighed. "Why try it again? You know they will bar the door. The rule says: NO WOLVES ALLOWED! You know that means you."

"I'll never give up on books," he declared. "Never!"
Then Winston smiled. "Do you suppose your grandmother's clothes might fit a wolf?"

Rosie scratched her head. "Grandma's clothes?"

"Trust me," said Winston. "I have a plan."

On Saturday morning at quarter to ten, Winston and Rosie walked to town. Winston wore a long, frilly, rose-print dress with ruffled lace at the neck. The skirt almost hid Winston's bushy tail and a floppy hat disguised his wolf-ly ears.

Perched on Winston's pointed snout were Grandma's specs in thin, wire frames.

When Winston and Rosie
arrived, no one blocked the
library door. Winston stuck his
snout inside and breathed in
the musty-dusty smell of books.

The librarian jumped to her
feet and stared. That grandma
looked familiar . . .

Rosie marched right up to her.
"I'd like you to meet Granny
Winston," she said. "She
needs a library card so she
can check out books. And
she'll gladly read at Story
Time – the children will love
her tales."

Winston nodded.
"I'll read to the children
all day long, if you like."

And so it was, week after week, "Granny Winston" read stories to children. If anyone noticed the sharp, white teeth, no one complained. And if at times the hem of Granny's skirt seemed to twitch and sway, no one revealed the secret.

Winston the Wolf – or Granny, so called – never lost his taste for words. Words were always and ever his favourite treat!

Winston
the
Book Wolf

Marni McGee & Ian Beck

the
Story
Lady

A NOTE TO THE READER:
If your Story Lady wears long
skirts and floppy hats, she may
be a Wolf in Disguise – a lover
of words, a gobbler of books.
Please be very kind – for me!

Love,

Winston the Wolf x